Black Stars in a White Night Sky

Black Stars
IN A
White Night Sky

JonArno Lawson

ILLUSTRATED BY Sherwin Tjia

WORDSONG

Honesdale, Pennsylvania

Originally published in Canada by Pedlar Press, 2006

Text copyright © 2006 by JonArno Lawson
Illustrations copyright © 2006 by Sherwin Tjia
All rights reserved
Printed in China
Designed by Helen Robinson
First U.S. edition, 2008

LIBRARY OF CONGRESS CATALOGING-IN-PUBLICATION DATA
Lawson, JonArno.
Black stars in a white night sky / by JonArno Lawson ;
illustrated by Sherwin Tjia. — 1st U.S. ed.
p. cm.
ISBN 978-1-59078-521-8 (alk. paper)
1. Children's poetry, Canadian. I. Tjia, Sherwin, ill. II. Title.
PR9199.3.L3395B55 2008

811'.54—dc22   2007018927

WORDSONG
An Imprint of Boyds Mills Press, Inc.
815 Church Street
Honesdale, Pennsylvania 18431

For Sophie, Asher, Samuel, Jacob, and Zoe

Contents

Contents

Contents

we is marchin'

Nature is a copiously
Hopeful cornucopia
Of protoplasmic organisms
Groping for utopia.

—E. Y. "Yip" Harburg

An Adventure Begins

An adventure begins,
when the one who was grimacing
suddenly grins.

An adventure begins,
when the one who was losing
suddenly wins.

An adventure begins,
when the one who acts saintly
suddenly sins.

When the smooth surface pops up with circling fins,
when soft drums surrender to bold violins,
when the light of the moon starts to shine on our skins,

an adventure begins.

Are You Worried?

Are you worried you're not
like everyone else?
Your worries will only worsen
when you find
that the path to conformity
is different for each person.

Love

She came round the corner and
all of a sudden
I understood it:

all love is sudden.

Golden Legs

Some go from shore to the deepest deep
one step at a time on their own two feet,
and so went Golden Legs.

Down she went
and back she came,
to the beach
and the glittering sky.
She rose and sank
like Hobbledy's flame,

the sea roared in, and she said good-bye—
as off again, on her own two feet,
in her own good time,
to the deepest deep,

went beautiful Golden Legs.

Mable leaves
the maple leaves
she's raking in a pile

to make believe
she's Cleopatra
sailing up the Nile.

You may believe
the maple leaves
that Mable leaves
are make-believe

but I believe
the maple leaves
that Mable leaves
are real.

And ever since she ran from them
I've been the one who's raking them—
I can't believe that you believe that
I would dream of faking them.

So maybe leave
what you believe
out of this entirely

and imagine for a moment
how badly I must feel

when you say
that you believe
the maple leaves
that Mabel leaves

aren't real.

Bartleby

If you see Bartleby
give me some warning—
Bartleby startles me
every morning.

Though I keep meaning
to ask him to stop,
I'm always too startled,
so I've given up.

The days have names,
the months have names,
and so do clouds and hurricanes.

But not the weeks:
of weekly names
nobody speaks—

it doesn't seem to bother us
that weeks pass by,
anonymous.

Black Stars in a White Night Sky

An empty cradle starts to cry;
why does no one stop it?
A cloud of bone goes rolling by
as if somebody'd dropped it.

And now you'd like to know how I
saw black stars in a white night sky.
I set my inward-gazing mind
reversing through my outward eye.

You can do it, too, now

try.

Etobicoke

You might think that Etobicoke
rhymes with words like *bloke* or *soak*—
but no, it rhymes with *blow*, or so
you'll be informed by Etobicoke folk.

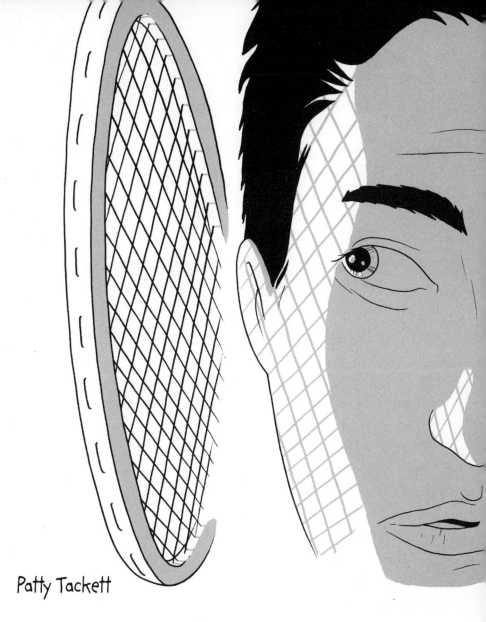

Patty Tackett

Patty Tackett
held a racket
right beside my head.
"Move it once and,
boy, I'll whack it,"
Patty Tackett said.

So I stood there
very still—
(stillness is a kind of skill)—
till, motionless,
I broke the will

of crazy Patty Tackett.

Being Thoughtless

I try to leave all
thoughts behind me,
but they always know.

They start to search
and start to find me
everywhere I go.

Is being thoughtless such a crime?
My thoughts seem
to think so.

Elephant

An eloquent elephant
out of its element
said things that others found Mad but Intelligent.

The elephant said, "You may find
me Inelegant,
but I'd rather seem out of my mind
than Irrelevant."

Frog on the Cob

I stopped at the door with my hand on the knob,
I felt a small jump in my throat.
My heart and my stomach were starting to throb,
I tried to rebutton my coat.

I started to turn—could I still get away?
My foot touched the uppermost stair—
but the door, it creaked open—she saw my sad face—
though she misunderstood my despair:

"What a long day you've had
at your horrible job!
But I've made your old favorite, love—
frog on the cob. …"

I can't stand the smell of it,
cannot think well of it,
live with the hell of it
day after day.
Genetically mutated
corn-based amphibian
chokes all my happiness—
speeds my decay.

But I turned with a smile,
said, "Hip, hip, hooray!
My favorite!
I'll savor it—
come straight away
and give me a pile,
the biggest green blob that you have,
of your marvelous
frog on the cob."

Humpty Dumpty

Humpty Dumpty
hid himself
underneath a chicken:

"I'm far from a wall,
so how can I fall?
I'll never again be stricken

by sad misfortune
or bad luck;
if I fall from this nest
I'll get right back up. ..."

But then something inside of him started to stir—
he had no idea
what was bound to occur
with that chicken on top of him,

though he knew something odd
was tapping about
right under his fragile skin.

He had no idea,
not the faintest idea,
of the danger
he was now in.

And before the poor fellow
could figure it out,
before he could reason
or voice a doubt,

a crack appeared in his neck—

and he broke apart from within.
Peck peck.

Thomas's Promises

Doubting Thomas
made a promise
that he couldn't keep.

I'd like to know
why Thomas is
breaking all his promises.

I'd also like to know
just what the secret
of his calmness is—

if I broke all my promises,
I'd worry
more than Thomas is.

Just look at it:
hard to remember,
now the days
have gotten colder

this bare gray hill
that I once loved
was at one time
autumn's shoulder.

A Bison in a Basin Playing a Bassoon

A bison in a basin
playing a bassoon
undertook to play the very
saddest sort of tune,

which broke the brittle nerves of a
Bavarian baboon,
who listened from a treetop
one depressing afternoon.

"Oh bison, stop reprising
that dismal melody.
Another beastly bar of it
will be the end of me!"

The bison, rising up, boomed,
"A baboon who disapproves?
Not just any cow can play bassoon
with cloven hooves.

"Behold, baboon, appreciate
the wonder of this sight—
a humble so-called buffalo
who gets each note just right!

"And you—tree-dwelling, foul-smelling
pseudo-troglodyte—
dare to ask me to refrain?
It's worse than impolite.

"Go leaping with the leopards, sir,
be gone now from my sight."

Gluts and scarcities,
scarcities and gluts,

once you've had a little bit
a little's not enough,

and once you've gotten used to it,
you just can't give it up.

You never compromise on it,
you tire out your eyes on it,

till one eye never opens
and the other never shuts.

Gluts and scarcities,
scarcities and gluts.

You Go, Hugo

You go, Hugo,
I'm all done—
but if you do go,
Run! Run! Run!

And if you, too, go?
Please, when you go,
do go say
hello to Hugo.

I Practiced

I practiced in the shower.
I practiced in the car.
I practiced in a downtown
karaoke sushi bar.

I practiced in the basement.
I practiced in my head.
I practiced on my bicycle.
I practiced in my bed.

But the fact is,
though I act as
if I practice
all the time,
it still seems
I'm either
stuck before
or getting past
my prime.

I practiced in the darkness.
I practiced while I read.
I practiced full of confidence,
I practiced full of dread.
I practiced for the living,
I practiced for the dead—

maybe I practiced
when I should have just been doing it
instead?

I Followed Your Tame Movements

I followed
your tame movements
with tame movements
of my own

(know now that all
my finest, wildest movements
came from your careful
slow improvements).

Deer

Deer delve deeper,
peer between endless greens,
gentle breezes tremble the reeds,
tempers seethe,
regrets deepen.

Whenever we freeze,
then flee—
whenever we're tender,
then severe—

we resemble deer.

It had to be gotten
and nobody was getting it,
nobody was letting it sink in—

and soon we'll be forgetting it—
what nobody is getting.
Although it might seem rotten,

I really can't help betting
that what nobody's letting
sink in will be forgotten.

Eat a Duck

Eat a duck, *quack-quack*,
eat a duck, *quack-quack*,
when you're hungry and you really need a snack,
quack-quack.

When you've fizzled and you're knackered
and they're calling you a slacker,
there's nothing like a quacker on a cracker.
Quack.

Water Waltz

Look how your
lovely face exalts
when you
forget about my faults.

Suddenly,
accepting me,
your lovely face
reflecting me,

your body vaults!

And diving in with somersaults,
you find the surface of my skin and join me
in my water waltz.

I confess, though it's a mess,
I've always liked this planet best.
While nothing here is infinite,
and I know only bits of it,

and what I know, I barely know—
life and death go on exchanging
death for life and life for death—
all the pieces fall apart, and reconverge with every breath.

Though ways to an answer have never been shut,
figuring out this strange world will never
be anything less than or anything but
a forever and ever endeavor.

There's a Worm

There's a worm
in the apple of my eye.
I saw its head emerge
and then retreat.

That monster with
its hundred shifting feet
begins the rot,
and soon the rot's complete.

My love, when comes the inborn urge to eat,
never eat yourself up from within:
eventually you'll
eat right through your skin.

Be patient with yourself,
begin again.

He leaps like spit
off a frying pan—
like hail off the lid
of a garbage can—

Kit kiddle knickerbocker
Rick a back rong.

And he jumps like jacks
off an open palm,
like a sapper
springs from a fizz-bang bomb—

Hit fiddle nikabrik
Bricabrac bong

Hip-hop handsome Han!
Hip! Hop! Boom! Bam!

And if you were born
with a danger horn,
then blow it
as hard as you can.

And if you were born
with a heart that was torn
back to where
the world began—

Fit a stick rack nickel
ipecac pong—

watch that handsome Han!

Hip! Hop! Boom! Bam!

He was here when the world began;
if he can't cure you, no one can.

You're big—why aren't you strong? And if you're quick, why do you always take so long? And if you have your own ideas, why do you always join the throng? And if you're the one who's smart—how come you're always wrong?

Ingomar Baltazar Caiaphas Copps

Ingomar Baltazar Caiaphas Copps
inched his way up to the toppermost tops,
wherever he's going he goes till he stops,
then bounds away homeward with backward hops.

In the Time That It Takes

In the time that it takes
for an eye to wink
for a wheel to turn
for a match to burn
for a stone to sink

for fingers to snap
for a kind thought to pass
for a roll in the grass
for a drop to drip
from the sky to your lip.

In the time that it takes
for a good-bye kiss
for a bird to hop
for a stone to skip
for a crow to deceive
for the mind to stop.
For the heart to believe.

In the time that it takes
for that same heart to break
for the sleeping to wake
for a dream to die
for a tear to fall
from your eye
to mine.

The First Real Warmth

Dead leaves
and seeds
winter inters:
with the first real warmth

what's dead
falls apart,
what's living
stirs.

The Snake's Advice, or Advice from a Snake to a Protohuman

Don't forfeit four feet
unless you get more feet,
no don't forfeit four feet
for two.

For once you're up standing
the world's more demanding—
slide down on your tum
and glide through.

How Without Arms

How, without arms,
did the sun
climb over the trees?

And without knees
to sink on,
how did it sink behind them?

And without eyes,
how did it peek
through the leaves?

And without
being wakened,
how did it rise?

The Old Man's Lie

"The old-fashioned way of gathering electricity
was to rub your shoes across a rug
and let the current
run down your fingers into a bucket:

"once full, you'd go spill it into the
central socket at the hub of the house.
I haven't done it for years.
Let's see if I still can. ..."

The old man
rubbed his slippered feet across
the rug, then touched the child's head.
A small spark jumped.

"You give it a try. ..."
He listened, full of doubt,
to the old man's lie
but felt the tiny spark,
and believed.

Old Man Margulis

Old man Margulis
throws cake to the pigeons:
he claims that their feelings get hurt
by the same old dull bread crumbs and sunflower seeds—
"What they coo for, my friends,
is dessert."

Clam

The clam appears calm
because it can't move,
but none really know how it feels.

It may seem to cope
with apparent aplomb
while wishing to take to its heels

when the snapping shrimps come
with the moon snails and whelks
to turn placid clams into meals.

I think that we all should admire the clam
for the fears
that it bravely conceals,

if indeed they are fears
that it bravely conceals

(for none really know how it feels).

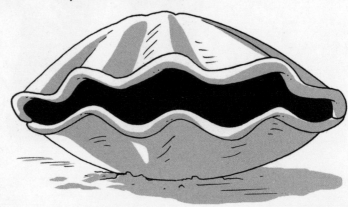

The upstarts
smack their wings
flat on the lake,

foolish feet
bob above,
wobble out straight,

their pencil-thin
shadows shoot over
like arrows.

And the slapped-at fish
flit back from the rock-fisted murk to watch the departures.

Hearing the last waterlogged honk of a solitary goose,
they dust below the surface with their fins,
and their silvery skins
hog the sun like falling coins.

Music Lessons at the Hamilton Armories

He practiced on his chanter,
tapping holes
with frozen fingertips above the gym,
a little Scotsman cultivating him
to someday don the pipes.

But was he worthy?
No, but was he worried?
No,
he'd never felt in any hurry
to give himself,
before his self was ripe.

The castigating Scotsman
gave up hope,
but from his resignation
there awoke
a new hope in the boy.

The chanter came to life now
in his hands.
When freed from outside hope
and hope's demands,
the notes rose where the old enchantment broke.

The stars, if they could notice,
would have noticed
the piper milking chimneys
of their smoke,
and if they could have heard
they would have listened
to the happy Scot's approbatory croak.

Winsome Billy Willoughby's
been wandering in the wood.
"The Wudu-Wasa's somewhere here—
he's much misunderstood,"

said winsome Billy Willoughby,
who hoped to do some good
explaining this weird wodwo
to the frightened neighborhood.

It snorted sharply
through its snout
when it caught sight of Billy,
and Billy felt a twinge of doubt:

was he being silly?
"The Wudu-Wasa's
truly good,
he's just been much misunderstood."

The Wudu-Wasa pawed the ground
and then it started growling.
And Billy thought, "How is it
it can smile while it's howling?"

His stomach tightened. "That's no good,
perhaps it's time to leave the wood?

"What does the Wudu-Wasa want?"
He never understood.
The Wuda-Wasa whooped and hollered,
but it did no good.

Whatever it was saying,
it remained misunderstood.
And after trying harder than perhaps
he might or should,

winsome Billy quickly left the Wasa's
neighborhood.

Pembroke had a cat who spoke,
but Pembroke didn't care.
It spoke to him of its nine lives
while Pembroke stroked its hair.

"Dear Cat," he said,
when the cat was done,
"I fear I lost track
after life number one."

The cat said, "Dear Pembroke,
I fear I'll start scratching
if you don't quit your habit
of rudely detaching."

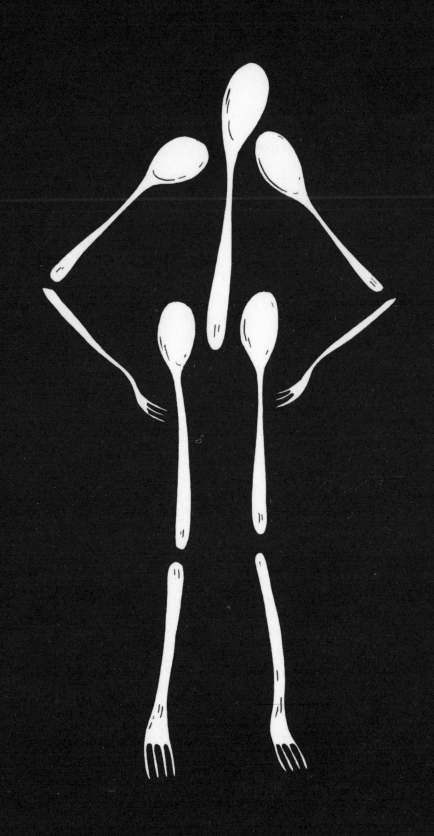

Skeletax

Before, though much like me and you,
he was already thin.
He'd say, "Food takes too long to eat,
and really, who needs skin?"

So Skeletax stopped eating and
got day by day much thinner.
He skipped breakfast, lunch, and snacks
and never ate his dinner.

"There's just no time,"
said Skeletax, though hunger made him grumpy,
and sitting on his bony bum
would sometimes make him jumpy.

Then, when his flesh was finally gone,
he never ceased his smiling,
a lipless moonless-midnight grin that
some found quite beguiling.

I found his smile insincere,
I knew he meant to flummox
those who say that none can live
with nothing in their stomachs.

Myself, I like the company of
those who like to eat.
Skeletax I leave to those
who'd rather self-deplete.

Neville

Neville never
really knew
what narishkeit
people put him through—

if you said it,
he'd believe it.
If you threw it,
he'd retrieve it.

Poor old Neville—
on the level—
docile, dear,
without a clue.

What's Left of Me?

What's left of me?
What's right of me?
You're hungered by the
sight of me.
I need what's left,
so do what's right
and please don't take
another bite.

Diving for Treasure

Her fair freckled face
sparkled bright
as a carnival

buffed by the crush
of the
cornicled deep—

she'd barked
her bare knuckles
on bevies of barnacles

waking a wreck
from
its coral-torn sleep.

An eerie unquiet
had scarred
all its treasure—

and though she could see
it held wealth
beyond measure

she left it behind for the ocean to keep.

The Peppercorn

The peppercorn is quite forlorn—
it's destined to be ground,
unless another home for it
is very quickly found.

"Oh me, oh my,"
sighed the peppercorn,
"I wish, like the salt,
that I'd never been born.

"I wasted my youth
on the Malabar Coast,
on a pepper plant
tied to a pepperplant post.

"If I'd shaken myself,
then I might well have dropped
and I'd …"
But the voice of the peppercorn stopped.

It fell in a sprinkling
of savory dust:
when it comes to good taste,
life is often unjust.

The Song That Turned into a Witch

By some preternatural sorcerous glitch,
the song I was singing turned into a witch—
a witch oh a witch of the wennechichenne,
she said, "I'm all ears and can always tell when a

"conjuring song gets infernal antenna
to gather me back from the infinite black—
and now let me warn you—don't get a word wrong,
one slip, and I'll turn straight back into a song."

But seeing as I had no wish to prolong
her visit with me (she would never belong),
I let my tongue slip: with a Hadean yip,
she vanished back into that unholy song.

And this is the song the enchantress resides in—
(some say *resides* and others say *hides* in):
when singing it make sure to make a mistake,
for she's listening, waiting, and always awake.

And now for the brave who don't fear being hexed,
the unholy Hornicle Song's coming next:

The Hornicle Song

Hornicle Bornicle
Gwidden, my sweet,
you came on a broom
and I came on my feet.

I knew what you were,
but I couldn't resist
when your moon-haloed silhouette
rose from the mist—

terrible voices
from the beyond—
the daft and the desperate
dare to respond.

Hornicle Bornicle,
demon's delight,
to ride on your broom with you,
holding you tight.

Oh, heaven be warned
and the devil beware,
when my face buries deep
in the thick of your hair—

terror at twilight
and danger at dawn—
the deft and the devilish
dare to go on.

Hornicle Bornicle,
why did we part?
There's no way to end it,
so why did we start?

I look at the sky
and I ache and I yearn,
but I know in my heart
that you'll never return—

terror at twilight
and danger at dawn—

the dim and the diligent,
brusque and belligerent,
duped and indifferent,
dare to go on.

Thirsty Kirsten

Thirsty Kirsten
took a sip
from the hip flask
on her hip.

Then she took
a second slug,
then a third,
then—chug-a-lug—

it was all gone,
she was bereft—
of hope for more,
there was none left.

But thirsty Kirsten's
awful thirst,
so oddly awful,
got much worse.

Thirst came first
with thirsty Kirsten,
she was just that kind
of person—

when her thirst
seemed at its worst,
it always found new ways
to worsen.

Crepe Eaters

They eat their crepes
behind drawn drapes,
they sneeze and cough
politely.

How quickly they
avert their eyes
from anything
unsightly.

Whatever happens,
good or bad,
they take it
very lightly.

Merciful Percival
took his submersible
down
where the killer whales weep,

where felonious lobsters
repentantly meet
other less famous crustaceous
submarine mobsters,

and guilt-ridden
gully fish creep.

But where each fish's viciousness
heightens each dish's deliciousness,
death can be sweet:
in the sea, life is tasty but cheap.

Yet down came old Percival
in his submersible,
somber, sincere, and discreet,
and there he performed many merciful acts,
which impressed those who weren't sound asleep.

But others detested him, said pride infested him,
felt that he dealt in deceit—
and rejecting his clemency, clung to his sub,
for it seemed like a good thing to keep.

They gripped it and bonked it and clipped it and conked it,
till Percival's mercy wore thin.
He said, "If I ever get out of this mess,
I will never have mercy again."

"In fact," said that peppery postulant, Percy,
"if I get away, I'll reverse all my mercy!"

But the ones who now clung to his hirpled submersible
reminded poor frustrated unlucky Percival
that merciful acts are, in fact, not reversible.

Moral:

The nethermost deep is not safely traversable.
Stay in the shallows when you're feeling merciful.

Silly Sally

Silly Sally,
don't sully your name—
if you didn't do it,
then don't take the blame.

Nothing Moves

Out on the cobblestones
trots an old hobble-boned horse
on its stone-clopping hooves.

The smoke's licking up
at the cracks in the bricks
and the cat's meowing round at the roofs.

And a dog's barking up at the darkening clouds—

but aside from the horse
and the smoke
and the cat
and the dog
and the clouds—

nothing moves.

I nicked my knuckle
on my buckle
fastening my belt;

my belt was holding up my pants;
my pants
were made of felt;

the shirt
that I tucked into them
was made from Georgia cotton,

but what does it matter about the rest
when the buckle I have
is rotten?

The Tines of a Fork

The tines of a fork,
the bowl of a spoon,
the edge of a knife,
a sliver of moon.

Top of a table—
and leg of a chair—
wick of a candle,
a locket of hair.

Stars coming over—
lamps going out—
an intimate whisper,
a faraway shout.

A half-open window,
a sash-tapping drape,
a half-asleep dreamer
who dreams half-awake

of the flight of a stork
arriving in June
by the side of his wife
with a sliver of moon.

Bringing Baby Home

I was watching the first time sunlight
touched her face on Murray Street,

rolling out of the clouds, dropping
to sleep on her sleeping cheek.

She'd never been away, never been home. The world
    was full of firsts,
changing itself forever for her. Renewed by her little
    long-fingered hands

moving carefully across the air
like starfish,

busy remaking the world.

Sleeping with the Baby

I'm sleeping with the baby in the day
because the baby will not sleep at night.
He's still too small to smile, or to play,
he's still too small to hold his head upright.

He purses up his lips in little *o*'s,
he nurses bit by bit, and then he goes
and grows and grows and grows and grows and grows.
How big he'll finally be, nobody knows.

For sore eyes he's a very lovely sight.
His brows are worried, but his face is bright.
I love him and his toothless hungry bite,
although he keeps us up, night after night.

Night after night, oh God, night after night.

A Girl in a Rabbit Hat

A girl in a rabbit hat
hopped round her habitat
huffing and puffing quite horribly.

A rabbit observing
said, "Girl, stop unnerving me,
please! You are hopping deplorably."

The girl said,
"Dear rabbit, when you get upset,
your nose wiggles very adorably."

Poor old Plotz,
why do you plummet
every time
you reach the summit?

It seems to me
the long way back
is much less painful.
Do you lack

the needed patience
for descent?
Or does your foot
just circumvent

the perch or cleft
for which it's searching?
Either way
you go off lurching

every time
you reach the top—it
sets a bad example.
Stop it.

The Fish

We lay half-asleep,
half-awake, on a mile-long shifting sheet
of sun-warmed sand,

when suddenly a wave
lifted and flipped
a twenty-pound carcass
of rotting fish-flesh at our feet.

It was all eyes
all spine
seeming desperate to be dead.

We turned about for help
twisted even
stood
but none was coming.

I searched for a stick
to dig with,
you fumbled after old boards,

together we dug
and buried it,
but it wouldn't rest,
couldn't stay down.

The waves remembered too—
and kept
finding it—

up it came back at us.

Finally we made it
a deep and decent grave
and even lodged
the board upright,
humming dumbly in the wind
as a warning to wanderers

and other
shore-heading waves
and carcasses.

We relaxed, but
too soon:
a boy saw the board.

He grasped it,
and yanked—
we yelled at him.

He dropped it.

His lips crawled open but the wind caught at them,
groped out his voice, stripped off the words,
and blasted them back,
garbling them down into his throat.

He tried again,
but the wind stiffened and smote,
boiled and broke over till he bent about,
irreparable,
and choked.

We couldn't understand him.
Finally his mother came
cursing
and turned him firmly back.

By the end of the day
the fish was up again,
wind rubbing gently now at the rot
of its dredged-up
death-drubbed grimace.

Its lidless and
skeletonized remnants
seemed less insistent,

the waves had receded—
there seemed no point in
further burial.

We left it to the crabs
and other small mechanics
of the sand.

Try saying this with any name you know,
and say it quickly:

Jim Flim tee-allago whim
tee-leggèd toe-leggèd bow-leggèd Jim.

Glen Fen tee-allago wen
tee-leggèd toe-leggèd bow-leggèd Glen.

Julie Shmoolie tee-allago woolie
tee-leggèd toe-leggèd bow-leggèd Julie.

Stephen Even tee-allago weeven
tee-leggèd toe-leggèd bow-leggèd Stephen.

And try to say these
over and over quickly:

1. Rain drops drop from treetops
Just like tea drops drip from teapots.

2. Exactly, it's ugly.

Pat a Snake

Pat a snake, pat a snake,
fakir's man,
wake me a snake as fast as you can—
pipe it out, raise it,
and when it's up ask it
if it really likes
being charmed from its basket.

I Had a Dream in Pittenweem

I had a dream in Pittenweem
of Isabel Goodsir Lonie
riding up from the sea
with a basket of fish
on William Robertson's pony—

"Are you well, Isabel?"

"How do I seem?
I'm trying not to brood:
I'll cease to exist
at the end of your dream,
and it's ruining my mood. ..."

Juliette from Baldicocks

"I'm Juliette from Baldicocks,
but everywhere I go, they mix me up with Goldilocks,
they do it even though
I never take a step without my handsome Romeo."

Said Romeo, "It's true, they mix her up with Goldilocks.
It doesn't make much sense—my Juliette from Baldicocks
has never, ever sought the kind of fairy-tale-ish dangers
that come from lying in the beds of hungry, furry strangers,

"or at least
not as far as I know,"
said her handsome
Romeo.

Schirokauer

Schirokauer had
just one eye,
he lost the other
in the sky
during an airplane battle—

out it went
and away he flew.

And strange to tell,
the eye he lost,
and not the one
he kept,
was the one the world
gazed into.

Tsunami

The wave travels silently
without companions,
gathering them into itself.

Passing through
everything
like a ghost,

it rushes with something
to tell the shore.
But by the time it arrives

it can only roar.

He Laughed with a Laugh

He laughed with a laugh
that he wished was his laugh,
but everyone knew it wasn't.

When he laughed he would ask,
"Does that sound like my laugh?"
And everyone said, "It doesn't."

The laugh that he laughed
that wasn't his laugh went,
"Hardy har har, guffaw!"

The laugh that he laughed
that he wished wasn't his went,
"Hruck, sniffle-hick, hee-haw!"

Hummingbird

Hummingbird's tumbling,
hummingbird's lunging,
sunlit fruit's luring—
hummingbird's

P
  L
    U
      N
        G
          I
            N
              G
                !

Faster and faster and faster she went,
and all she rolled over got broken and bent.
Who on earth was she and why was she sent?

Though many were questioned, nobody knew,
but the faster she went, the bigger she grew,
and the bigger she grew, the faster she went—

some gathered to wonder at what it all meant
and others to ask what she might represent,
but still none could guess what might be the intent

of her surging and burgeoning whirling descent,
none could make sense of it, none could prevent
the flattening violence the world underwent,

till someone threw up a great wall of cement,
right in the path of the way she was headed,
and that's where she stopped at last, slightly imbedded.

Then a laugh was heard, "Excellent! Just what I needed!
I wanted to stop—now I've finally succeeded!
And look, I've gone back to my regular size!"

And when she rose up, she looked so angelic it
seemed that to chastise her would be indelicate.
Right then they decided they might as well hide it—

and so they concealed from the innocent, guiltless
(though none would say harmless), and guileless girl,
their flattened, destabilized, half-destroyed world.

Handsome Prince

"Go on, kiss her,
handsome prince, don't treat it like a duty!
What man wouldn't envy you
for kissing Sleeping Beauty?"

"I'm sorry, but I can't,"
the handsome prince said, eyes a-twinkle.
"My heart, my soul, and waking kiss
belong to Rip Van Winkle."

Bigger and Better

I'm going to do something bigger and better,
bigger and better
and bolder, but first,
I'm going to do something
smaller and worse.

Fly, Lynx

Lynx— "Fly, fly."

Fly— "Why, lynx?"

Lynx— "Try."

Fly— "Why try?"

Lynx— "Shy, fly?"

Fly— "Shy??!! *Bzzzzzz! Zm! Zm! Zm!*"

Lynx— "Tsk tsk! My my!"

Tickle Tackle Botticelli

Tickle tackle Botticelli
chirping cockatoo
chock-a-lick a chocolate drop
kockamamie moo.

Chomp alompa omphalos
charber choparoo.
Listen up and look around and
think a little, too.

A click and a clack,
a blip in the black—
a jittery dog
on a dock—

can you remember
how you thought
before you
learned to talk?

Consider that, consider this,
consider it on the dot,

that words, however used,
are just the playthings
of a thought.

Some small-type notes
for those with excellent eyesight

An Adventure Begins When my daughter was born, I wrote to tell my friend Aubrey Davis. "An adventure begins!" was his response. When I asked him about it later, he didn't remember writing it.

Etobicoke My friend Amanda Sue Ross, a lifetime Torontonian, mispronounces Etobicoke (the name of one of Toronto's boroughs) deliberately (I think?), which gave me the idea.

Frog on the Cob When he was a year and a half, my son had a pair of frog-patterned pajamas—we called them his froggy jammies. He repeated this as "Cobby Nannies." When I heard him say this, I suddenly had an image of a pulsating frog attached to a corncob.

Gluts and Scarcities I came across this phrase in the nineteenth-century *Ordnance Survey Memoirs of Ireland*.

I Followed Your Tame Movements For Amy.

I've Always Liked This Planet The image of the world disintegrating and being remade with every breath is a paraphrase of a passage in Sirdar Ikbal Ali Shah's book *Islamic Sufism*.

There's a Worm The line "There's a worm in the apple of my eye" came from a film script about a manipulative high-school teacher, which I was trying to write with my friend Alex Chapple ten or so years ago.

Hip-Hop Handsome Han My children—in the tub, in the car, during any lull in a conversation—demand *Star Wars* stories. The only rule is that my wife and I are not allowed to use the plots from the movies—the characters must have new experiences all the time. Hip-Hop Handsome Han emerges from one of these ridiculous bathtub tales, where the hip-hop dancing of Handsome Han the Dancin' Man impresses Jabba so much that Jabba frees him from his dungeon. Nikabrik is the name of a bad dwarf in C. S. Lewis's *Prince Caspian*. "If you have a danger horn, then blow it as hard as you can" is a phrase my daughter came up with one day.

Ingomar Baltazar Caiaphas Copps Ingomar was the name of my mother's high-school boyfriend. Baltazar was the name of a former basement tenant.

Old Man Margulis Taken from Nadezhda Mandelstam's biography of Osip Mandelstam, *Hope Abandoned* (pages 125–126). In addition to his adult works, Osip Mandelstam wrote light verse and children's poetry, none of which survived, aside from what Nadezhda records in her memoir. Osip and Nadezhda had a good friend named Ivan Margulis, and many of Osip's light-verse poems started with the words *Old Man Margulis*. The poems were written as a sort of game, which had only two rules: each poem had to start with the words *Old Man Margulis* and had to meet with the approval of Margulis himself.

Music Lessons at the Hamilton Armories One day, my son suddenly sang "The farmer milks the chimney" while he was singing "The Farmer in the Dell." When I showed this poem to my father, he wrote the following in response:

I think all springboards are internal,
that all of outside hope's infernal—
though heat, so roused, itself may cause
external products that will prove eternal

Winsome Billy Willoughby Ted Hughes's collection *Wodwo* is where I came across the wodwo (also known as the wudu-wasa—a satyr, faun, or wild man of the woods) for the first time. Hughes himself found the wodwo in *Sir Gawain and the Green Knight*.

Skeletax I made this up as a nonsense word, but I've since discovered that it's the Russian word for skeletons.

Neville *Narishkeit*, a term used in both Yiddish and German, means "nonsense" or "foolishness." It entered my everyday vocabulary through my mother-in-law, Sheila, and my wife, Amy.

Diving for Treasure How *bare knuckles* and *barnacles* might be used together in a poem was a problem that troubled me for years.

The Song That Turned into a Witch As I was trying to think of a name for this collection, my daughter said, "What about 'Itchity Pitchity Pitch, the Song Turned into a Witch'?" This poem grew out of her suggestion.

The Hornicle Song I borrowed the unusual last name Hornicle as a nonsense word from Thomas McGrath's *Letter to an Imaginary Friend*.

Merciful Percival *Hirpled* is a Scottish word for *hobbled*.

The Knuckle-Nicking Buckle I once nicked my knuckle on my buckle, just as described.

The Fish Based on a huge half-rotted fish that my brother and I were suddenly confronted with out of the waves on the shore of Assateague Island, Virginia. We tried, unsuccessfully, to bury it.

Try saying this with any name you know, and say it quickly This is a rhyme my father learned in Albany, New York, in the early 1930s.

I Had a Dream in Pittenweem Pittenweem is a town in Fife, Scotland. Isabel Goodsir Lonie and William Robertson are two of my Fifeshire ancestors.

Schirokauer Arno Schirokauer (1899–1954) was a German philologist, teacher, and writer. I was named in part for him. He really did lose an eye during a First World War air battle.

Tickle Tackle Botticelli *Charber* is a word my daughter made up and used to say to herself quite often. She also used to say "choplit chicks" for chocolate chips, but I couldn't work it into the poem. It became "Chock a lick a chocolate drop."

Deer, Hummingbird, and **Fly, Lynx** are all lipograms. These poems also appear in my book *A Voweller's Bestiary*.

Acknowledgments

I am deeply indebted to my family—Amy, Sophie, and Asher—for being the first listeners and for generating and inspiring many of the ideas I pursued in this book. *Black Stars in a White Night Sky* could not have existed in its current form, and most of it would not have existed at all, without the generous support of the Canada Council for the Arts. Gratitude from the nethermost deep goes to Beth for her sensitive and intelligent handling of the work as a whole. Sherwin—where would it (and I) be without you? And thanks to Zab for her great, careful, wide-open eyes. I am also grateful to Louise Simpson and her finely made *Avid Hands Anthology* (Volume 2), in which an earlier version of "The Fish" first appeared. Thanks to Damian Lopes (and his company, Fingerprinting Inkoperated) for publishing an earlier version of "Love" entitled "All of a Sudden." "Tsunami" was done as a variation on Roald Hoffmann's poem by the same title, from his collection *Soliton* (Kirksville, MO: Truman State University Press, 2002). Thank you to the organizers and sponsors of gritLIT 2005 in Hamilton, Ontario, where I was able to try out many of these poems for the first time. And a final thanks to Next Decade Entertainment and Ernie Harburg for allowing the use of Yip Harburg's poem "WE IS MARCHIN'."

"WE IS MARCHIN'" by E. Y. "Yip" Harburg.
Published by Glocca Morra Music (ASCAP). Administered by Next Decade Entertainment, Inc. All rights reserved. Used by permission.